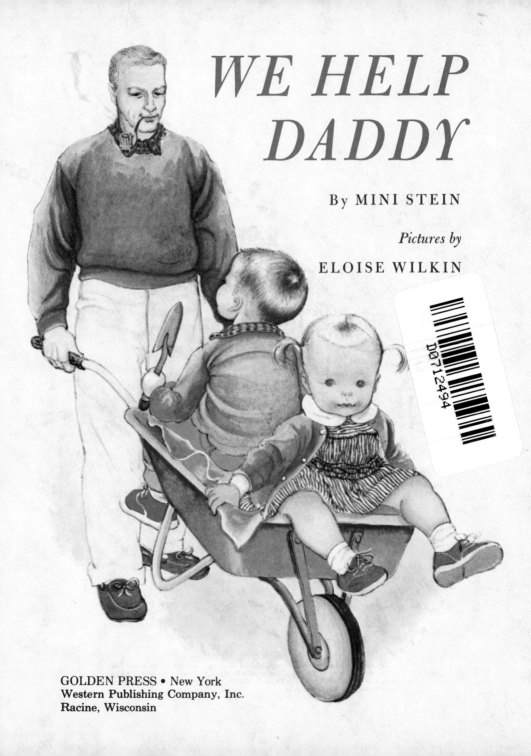

WE HELP DADDY

By MINI STEIN

Pictures by

ELOISE WILKIN

GOLDEN PRESS • New York
Western Publishing Company, Inc.
Racine, Wisconsin

The artist, Eloise Wilkin, would like to
say "thank you" to Cynthia and James
Kimble who posed for the pictures.

We help Daddy a lot, Benjy and I. Daddy fixes the attic door. He calls, "Hammer, please."

Benjy hands him the hammer.

Then Daddy says, "Sue, are you ready to help me, too?"

I am Sue, so I hold out my hands to show I am ready.

I bring the tin plate and Benjy puts the old rusty nails in it.

"You are a help," Daddy says to us.

In the garden Daddy and Benjy pull out weeds.

I pull out weeds, too. I see a nice little snail. When he sees me, the snail puts his head in, under his shell.

"Now we must water the plants," Daddy says.
Benjy turns on the faucet.
He helps Daddy water the big flowers.
I water the pink geranium with my very own little watering can.

"The hedge needs a haircut," Daddy says.

Daddy picks up the shears and clip, clip, clip
—the hedge is neat and tidy.

Benjy gathers the clippings and throws them
in the waste basket. I help him.

Our dog, Zip, needs a bath. His paws are muddy, and he has some burrs on his coat. Zip does not like baths. He runs away. Benjy and I catch him.

I wash his wiggly ears, Benjy soaps his curly coat. Daddy washes Zip all over.

Poor Zip looks so unhappy.

We splash warm water all over Zip and then
we rub him dry. Now Zip is nice and clean.

"The kitchen fence needs a coat of paint," says Daddy.

Benjy brings the paint brush. I spread newspaper so that Daddy can put the paint can on it.

We can see Mommy baking in the kitchen.
She waves to us and says, "Hello, busy bees..."

Daddy dips the brush in the can and paints
the rails.

I run and get my own little paint brush. Now
I can help, too.

"We have a new picture to hang," calls
Mommy.

We all go into the living room.

Benjy and I hold the picture up. Daddy puts
wire cord through the two rings.

Daddy climbs the step ladder. I give him a
hook to fix in the wall. Then up goes the picture.

"It's hanging all crooked," says Benjy.
Daddy straightens the picture and says,
"Thank you, Benjy."

Next we decide to make a bird feeder.
Daddy has a wooden tray for the bottom.
"I need two pieces for the sides," he says.
Benjy hands him the wood and Daddy saws
it in two.

I help Benjy keep hold while Daddy nails
one piece of wood on each side of the tray. Then
he nails the roof on and puts a big hook in it.

I put bread crumbs and seeds on the tray and we hang it near the kitchen window. We watch the birds eat.

"Let's get some logs for the fire," says Daddy.
Benjy and I push the wheelbarrow along.
Daddy chops the logs and we pile them in
the wheelbarrow and take them to the house.

Our next job is to clean the car. Daddy takes the hose and splashes the car all over.
Benjy and Daddy wipe it dry.
I help, too.

"Hmm, we need to polish," says Daddy.

Daddy polishes the front. Benjy polishes the sides. I polish the door handles.

"See how the car shines," says Benjy.

"I'm glad I've got such good helpers," says Daddy with a smile.

Last of all we have to mend the handle on Benjy's dresser.

"Where's the screwdriver?" asks Daddy. Benjy finds the screwdriver for Daddy.

Daddy takes off the broken handle and screws on the new one.

"Thank you, Daddy," says Benjy.

"Wash your hands for supper," Mommy calls.

Benjy sees a nail sticking out of the bathroom door.

"That must come out before someone gets hurt," says Daddy.

"I'll get the pliers," says Benjy, and Daddy
pulls the nail out.

"What would I do without my helpers,"
Daddy says to Mommy.

After supper we are very, very sleepy. We had such a busy day helping Daddy.

Mommy tucks us into bed and says, "Daddy and I are so pleased with our two helpers."

Benjy and I are very pleased, too. Helping Daddy is fun!